THE NIGHT CROSSING

The Night Crossing

by Karen Ackerman

illustrated by Elizabeth Sayles

Alfred A. Knopf • New York

THIS IS A BORZOI BOOK PUBLISHED BY ALFRED A. KNOPF, INC.

Manufactured in the United States of America
10 9 8 7 6 5 4 3 2 1

Library of Congress Cataloging-in-Publication Data
Ackerman, Karen, 1951–
The night crossing / by Karen Ackerman ;
illustrated by Elizabeth Sayles.
p.   cm.
Summary: In 1938, having begun to feel the persecution that all
Jews are experiencing in their Austrian city,
Clara and her family escape over the mountains into
Switzerland.
ISBN 0-679-83169-X (trade)
1. Holocaust, Jewish (1939–1945) —Juvenile fiction.
[1. Holocaust, Jewish (1939–1945)—Fiction. 2. Jews—
Austria—Fiction. 3. Austria—Fiction.]
I. Sayles, Elizabeth, ill. II. Title.
PZ7.A1824Ni 1994   94-10805
[Fic]—dc20

For CLARA, with remembrance,
for MIMI, with love, and
for the one and a half million children
who perished in the Holocaust

THE NIGHT CROSSING

1

One night, just after Clara and her older sister, Marta, were put to bed, Clara overheard her parents talking in the sitting room.

"We must leave Austria now, before it is too late," her father murmured.

Softly her mother replied, "But Innsbruck is our home, Albert."

It was 1938, and not too many

months earlier, there had been laughter, conversation, joking, and singing in their home. But the family piano had been sold to buy firewood, and now the only sounds Clara heard at night were the whispers of fearful voices.

"I won't let us be rounded up and sent to some prison that the Nazis call a camp," her father continued. "Jews get branded like animals, the rumors say. I will not allow it to happen!"

"But what will we do?"

"I'll make arrangements tomorrow," Clara's father said. "Austrian money can still buy a way for us to escape Hitler and his Nazis."

Though Clara didn't know quite what her father meant, she knew that since Adolf Hitler and the Nazis had invaded Austria from Germany, terrible things had been happening to the Austrian people, especially Jewish Austrians.

As she lay in bed, Clara held Gittel and Lotte, her two favorite dolls, tightly. At last she fell asleep.

"JUDEN! JUDEN!" a young voice screamed, joined by another voice, and then another, until the voices all came together in one thunderous roar behind them. Marta held Clara's hand so tightly that Clara nearly cried as the two sisters ran across the rough cobblestones of the street that led to their home.

They flew past the Duessel bakery, boarded up and painted with Nazi

swastikas, and they jumped over the trash that lay on the sidewalks of what had once been an orderly street of houses. Now the homes all had broken windows and looked empty even if they weren't. The Jewish families inside often lived in back rooms and basements, hoping to make a quick escape if the Nazi police appeared at their front doors.

Clara didn't have to turn around and look to know that among the group that was chasing them was her best friend, Hilde.

Marta pulled Clara up the front steps into the doorway of the building where they lived, and the other children scattered. The girls were safely inside, at least until school the next day.

*　　*　　*

CLARA WOKE SUDDENLY to Marta's grumbling.

"You kicked me again," Marta complained, turning on her side to go back to sleep. "You were dreaming."

The real chase had happened more than a week earlier, but Clara still dreamed of it. She got up from the bed with her two dolls in her arms.

"Mama?" Clara whispered as she entered the shadows of the sitting-room doorway.

Her mother looked up, startled, from where she sat in the candlelight because there was no money to pay for electricity. Lately, any little noise in the house alarmed Mama.

"Another nightmare?" she asked softly. Clara nodded. "Come, *maydel*," she said, and opened her arms to her younger daughter. Clara climbed onto her lap, and Mama pulled the edges of her shawl around them both.

"Will they take us away?" Clara asked.

Mama held her tightly. "I won't let anyone take you away—ever—so you mustn't worry."

"But they chased us, and the Nazis took Mr. Duessel. I saw them, Mama. They broke the windows of the bakery and went in and dragged him out to the street," Clara whispered. "They laughed when Mrs. Duessel begged them not to take him away, and one of them spit on her as they drove off."

Her mother did not answer. There was nothing to say, because it was all

true. The Duessel kosher bakery had been raided, and Mr. Duessel arrested for continuing to bake and sell kosher goods to Jews. The bakery had been boarded up, and Mrs. Duessel had gone to live with her daughter and son-in-law. No one knew where Mr. Duessel was now.

"If we're very careful, we'll all be fine," Mama finally replied. "Now go back to bed, Clara."

But as she slipped from her mother's lap and moved toward the room she shared with Marta, Clara could see the worry on her mother's face as she began to remove the yellow stars that were stitched to the tattered coats of her two daughters.

Climbing into bed, Clara arranged

Gittel and Lotte next to her beneath the covers. The dolls had once belonged to Clara's grandmother. They were very old and filled with straw. Each doll was dressed in the bright-colored apron and kerchief of a Russian peasant.

Clara's grandmother had told her that when she was a young girl, she had carried the dolls in her arms as her family made a night crossing. They had crossed over the Carpathian Mountains from their home in Russia to escape the Cossack armies that had burned Jewish houses and shops.

Her grandmother's family had to flee their Russian village because Jews were being beaten. In Russia this was called a pogrom.

"We had to leave everything behind

and run for our lives," Grandma had said. "But Gittel and Lotte were very brave, and they wanted to go along. So my mother let me carry them over the mountains and all the way to Austria."

"On your night crossing," added Clara.

"Yes, *maydel,* on my night crossing to freedom," Grandma replied as she put the two dolls in Clara's arms.

Now, as Clara drifted back to sleep in the dark, she hoped Papa would let her take Gittel and Lotte with her to wherever he planned to take the family to escape the Nazis.

2

few days later Clara's father began collecting all the family's valuables. He took a large pillowcase from Mama's linen drawer and led the family through each room to look for things that could be sold. To Clara it seemed almost like a game.

From the parlor he took the beautiful silver tea service he'd given Mama on their first wedding anniversary. From their bedroom Papa took his own pocket watch with its hand-engraved fob and all of Mama's jewelry, even her wedding ring. Clara and Marta followed him, looking for things to put into the pillowcase.

"Soon we'll begin our night crossing to Switzerland," Papa told them as he made his way to his daughters' room. "There, Jewish people are still free from the Nazi police. We're going to pretend that we have visited cousins here in Innsbruck and that we are Swiss citizens returning home," he explained.

Into the pillowcase went the Star of David on a gold chain that Marta had been given upon her graduation from the eighth grade. Marta frowned. She didn't want to leave the few friends she still had, and she didn't want to leave Innsbruck.

"But some people say that the Nazis won't stay for long, Papa," Marta softly protested.

"In Switzerland we can live a normal life while 'some people' wait to find out if the Nazis stay or not," Papa murmured, moving toward the dining room.

He picked up a small cut-glass dish and four brass napkin rings and dropped them into the pillowcase. But when he reached for the pair of old silver candlesticks, Mama stopped him.

"No, Albert! Please—anything, everything but these!" she said.

The candlesticks had been in Mama's

family for generations. They were nearly ten inches high, and candles were lighted in them before every Sabbath and on holidays. Clara and Marta had helped Mama polish them once a week for as long as they could remember.

"But Helen, these are worth a fortune," Papa gently argued. "And we'll never be able to hide them so that they won't be found."

Still Mama would not part with them. "That monster Hitler may take away everything else, but he won't have my entire family history!" Mama said.

So Papa left with the pillowcase of valuables under his worn coat to buy the arrangements for their escape to

freedom. Some of the money would be given to the people who would risk their lives just by helping the family along the way.

Watching Mama defend the candlesticks reminded Clara of the many Friday evenings they had spent together, gathered around the dining room table to celebrate the Jewish Sabbath. Mama always began the Sabbath by lighting the candles. She moved her hands in a small circle above the flame of each candle. Then she raised her hands and covered her eyes, as she recited the *bracha,* the Sabbath blessing.

Clara liked to say the blessing along with her mother. It began *"Baruch atah Adonai,"* and her mother's voice was always full of gentleness and love. But now there was a law that forbade Jews from celebrating the Sabbath or going to the synagogue.

By the time Papa returned home, the silver candlesticks had been sewn into the folds of Marta's heavy muslin petticoat. Papa shook his head but said nothing.

He pulled a handful of money from his coat pocket and laid the bills on the table. "From this moment, all of you must remember that we are no longer Austrians. We are citizens of Switzerland," he declared.

"Will we cross the mountains like Grandma did?" Clara asked excitedly. A night crossing seemed like a great adventure to her, and she was curious to see the high, snowy Alps that marked the border between Austria and Switzerland.

"Yes, like Grandma," Papa answered. "But we're pretending to have been visiting for just a few days, so Mama can pack just one satchel. We mustn't look like we are escaping, so you and Marta can take only what you can wear or put in your pockets. And remember that we'll be walking a very long way."

Marta frowned. She knew she would have to leave her new schoolbooks behind. Still, she was determined to find room for at least a few of them.

Clara looked through her wardrobe and tried to pick out the dress with the biggest pockets. At last she chose one that Grandma had made for her. It had two giant pockets on the top and a matching pinafore with pockets all across the bottom. She looked sadly at the small vanity table that Papa had bought used and refinished for her on her last birthday. Now it would never be covered with perfume bottles and tins of bath powder like Marta's table in the opposite corner. Silently Clara said good-bye to the vanity and to all of the things she would be leaving behind.

That evening the family sat down to a final supper in their Austrian home. Mama seemed nervous as she served the meal, but Papa looked happy for the first time in months.

He lifted a glass of water, which was all they had to drink.

"To our freedom," he toasted. "And to a safe night crossing."

Then, as Marta put her glass back down, they all heard the pair of silver candlesticks clink inside the folds of her petticoat.

3

Marta and Clara went to bed fully dressed in the clothes they would wear on their journey hours later. Slight shadows remained on each of their coats in the places where Mama had removed the yellow stars.

Clara's pockets took up a lot of room in the bed because she had tucked some hair ribbons and a tiny silver-edged mirror—as well as Gittel and Lotte—inside them. And Marta had a terrible time trying to fall asleep. The pockets and folds of her clanking petticoat were stuffed with Mama's candlesticks and a few very heavy hardbound schoolbooks.

It was still pitch dark outside when Papa woke them. Sleepily Marta and Clara rolled out of bed and followed him to where Mama waited near the cellar door, holding the family's only satchel.

"Absolute silence," Papa whispered as the four of them slipped out to the street.

The family walked and walked, past all the familiar houses and buildings in their neighborhood, being careful to

hide in whatever shadows the creeping sunrise left undisturbed. Quietly each of them said a silent, special good-bye to the city they loved, which was once beautiful but now looked so broken and beaten.

At last they reached a small farmhouse with a barn a few miles outside the city of Innsbruck. Papa led them silently into the barn, where they settled behind the protective cover of two large hay bales. Then Papa peered through the barn door carefully, stepped outside, and quickly made his way toward the house.

Both Clara and Marta were surprised that unlike the city, the Austrian countryside seemed untouched by the war. The fields and woods were still as lush as when their parents had brought Clara and Marta to the country for a picnic long ago. Each house had a small, steady stream of smoke rising from its chimney. It was as if the Austrian farmlands had not gone to war with the German army at all.

When Papa returned, he had a small cloth filled with goat cheese and hard brown bread. The two girls ate as much as they wanted, and then their parents finished what was left.

For an entire day they stayed hidden in the barn. When the two girls weren't sleeping, Marta read from the books she'd stuffed into her pockets, and Clara played with Gittel and Lotte. The night crossing wasn't so bad after all, Clara thought.

For hours Papa sat watching the farm road through the barn slats and studying the small map that the Resistance had drawn for him to show where it was safe—or nearly safe—for the family to walk.

Meanwhile, Mama gazed at the Swiss Alps in the distance. The Swiss border was still far away, and to reach it the family would have to climb over the steep, rocky foothills of one of the tallest mountain ranges in the world.

When the sun finally set, Papa led them from the barn to the thick woods beyond the farmhouse.

Every now and then the silver candlesticks clinked in their hiding place inside Marta's petticoat.

Again the family walked and walked

in the dark, past crop fields and cow pastures and hedgerows that barely provided them with cover from either the light of the moon or the bitter cold.

Clara's feet began to hurt, and then to swell, so Papa had to pick her up and carry her on his back. Marta and Mama looked more exhausted with every mile. All of them felt grumpy and tired, even Papa, who answered their questions about how much longer and how much farther they would have to walk with unusually sharp replies.

"Just walk," he told them. "Keep walking."

Once during the night the family had to hide quickly from Nazi armored tanks that roared past them on the road near the woods. Then they began to walk again.

When a small patrol suddenly appeared, Papa motioned to be quiet, and they all crouched behind some weeds at the side of the road.

A soldier came close and poked around with the bayonet at the end of his rifle. Peeking out from beneath her father's arms, Clara saw the moonlight reflecting off the bayonet's sharp blade.

The buttons on the soldier's uniform were polished brightly. As Clara caught a glimpse of his features, she was surprised that he was so young—not much older than the boys in their early teens who had just begun to court her sister Marta. He was just a boy, with fine blond hairs on his upper lip. A Nazi boy, with a gun.

Holding their breath, the family huddled motionless in the dark as the blade

of the bayonet plunged down, first in front and then behind them.

Finally the soldier turned away.

But Mama's stomach rumbled loudly from hunger, and each of them froze with fear. The soldier stopped and turned back toward the weeds, listening.

They waited for him to call out to his fellow soldiers, waited to be caught and taken away like the others.

But somehow the soldier changed his mind.

"*Ist nicht*," he called to the others. "It's nothing."

When the patrol had finally gone, Mama broke down in tears.

"It's all right, Helen, it's all right,"

Papa murmured, holding her. "We're all hungry, and empty stomachs don't know anything about Nazi patrols."

Now Clara understood how dangerous their night crossing was—and they hadn't even reached the slopes of the Alpine foothills yet.

4

The family continued to walk. Every mile was more difficult as they drew closer to the mountains. The air was thinner from the high altitude, and the steep angle of the path they followed was tiring. Clara's feet had swollen over the tops of her shoes, and she'd had to remove them, which hurt terribly. Though she tried not to, she cried now and then from the pain.

Finally, as dawn approached, they were able to stop and rest in a ramshackle goat shed, a hiding place that Papa had arranged for before they left Innsbruck. For a great deal of money, the man who owned the shed was willing to look the other way while they hid, in the cold straw among goat droppings, from the Nazi patrols.

But the family had been in the shed only a short time when the man who owned it threw open the latched door and motioned angrily to Papa.

The man spoke quickly and turned back toward his small house a few yards from the shed. Papa's shoulders slumped as he turned to his family.

"He wants more money—or he'll turn us in," Papa told them sadly. "He says the Nazi patrols have been searching his farm every now and then, and he won't continue to risk his family without more money." They all knew that the money Papa got for selling their valuables had already been spent.

"We're so close," Papa murmured to himself, shaking his head with worry.

Just then the shed door opened once more. It was a woman this time, likely the farmer's wife, with a small basket of food covered with a checked cloth. She smiled briefly at them and held out the basket to Mama. But Mama stared down at the dirt floor, so the woman turned to Marta and offered her the basket instead.

As Marta reached out, a slight clink sounded.

Mama looked up desperately, certain that her candlesticks would be the price of their hiding place. But Marta was no fool.

Quickly Marta jingled the links of a small moonstone bracelet on her arm. The bracelet was a present she'd received last Hanukkah from a classmate, and not valuable enough for Papa to sell with their other possessions.

. The early morning sun streamed through the reedy slats of the shed, and Marta purposely turned the bracelet a bit to catch the sunlight. The woman seemed to like the bracelet very much.

"Ah," she murmured with admiration as Marta took the basket from her.

When she reached out to touch the bracelet, Marta pulled her arm away, taking a chance that a show of selfishness would make the woman want the bracelet even more.

Though she had a safe home in Nazi territory, the farmer's wife looked desperate and poorer than the gentiles in Innsbruck. Her weary face showed that life in the countryside was indeed touched by war.

The woman stood straight, giving Marta an angry look, then turned and left.

"Good, Marta—very good!" Papa exclaimed, giving his older daughter a hug. "When she tells her husband about the bracelet, he'll know that a Nazi patrol wouldn't let him keep it if he turned us in. So he will have to bargain with us, or his wife will pester him!"

The family huddled together in the shed, and they waited. Then, as they had hoped, the man appeared at the door with his wife standing behind him.

So a deal was made, and Marta's moonstone bracelet was the price of hiding in the shed until sunset, when the family would continue on their night crossing.

Once again they'd been lucky.

5

When darkness fell over the hilly path that led to the Swiss border, the family crept quietly from the goat shed and out into the cold.

"The border is only two miles away," Papa told them, but the icy winds of the Alps were making two miles seem like a hundred. Clara wanted to walk on her own, with swollen feet covered only by cotton socks, but Papa continued to carry her.

Finally the path began to slope down toward the flatlands, and the night air seemed less chilled. Papa urged them on, tired but stern, snapping at Marta or Mama if they stumbled and fell. Finally they reached the base of the foothills, just a few hundred feet from the Swiss border.

But Nazi soldiers were guarding the border gate with rifles slung across their shoulders.

"We'll never get past them with those candlesticks banging!" Papa whispered urgently. "Even with false papers, we won't escape the racket they'll make! We have to leave them behind, Helen."

But Mama whispered just as urgently, "Those candlesticks are all I have left, Albert! I won't leave without them!"

"Well, there has to be a better hiding place than Marta's petticoat!" Papa snapped, though his expression softened as he began to look through the few belongings the family had with them. Still, nothing seemed as if it would do.

Just then Clara knew where the candlesticks would be safe.

"Will they fit inside Gittel and Lotte, Papa?" she asked, and she held out the dolls to her father. "They've made a night crossing before, and they aren't at all afraid!"

Papa stared at her. "I always knew the women in this family had the brains!" he said with a smile, and he took Gittel and Lotte from Clara.

Mama removed the candlesticks from Marta's petticoat, then made a hole in a side seam of each doll and emptied the straw filling onto the ground. She slipped a candlestick inside each doll's body and stuffed the remaining straw back in to fill out its shape. With a sewing needle she'd packed in the satchel, she stitched the same thread back over the seams. When Mama had finished sewing, Papa picked up Gittel, then Lotte, and gave each doll a good shake. The candlesticks inside could not be heard or felt.

"Are we ready, then?" Papa asked, and Clara, Marta, and Mama nodded. Then, looking down at Clara, Papa said, "You must carry the dolls, *maydel,* so the soldiers won't suspect. Can you be very brave?"

"Yes, Papa," she answered, and put Gittel and Lotte into her pockets. Her father reached down, took Clara's hand, and squeezed it. Then Clara and her family stepped out from behind the trees and made their way toward the border gate.

One of the young soldiers at the border gate rose from his wooden chair and stepped toward the family as Papa took their false papers from his coat pocket.

The soldier scanned the papers, looked at the family and scowled. Then he bent down to look in Clara's eyes.

"*Wohin gehen Sie?*" he snapped. "Where are you going?"

Clara felt her father's hand tighten around hers as she stared up at the soldier.

"I'm going home, sir, after a visit with my cousins in Innsbruck, Austria," Clara answered. "I'm a little homesick, although my cousins were very nice to me."

The soldier smiled and stood upright. He nodded and called to his fellow soldiers to open the gate.

But he kept looking at the dolls in Clara's pockets.

Clara held her breath as the wooden

gate rose. Just as the family was about to go through, the soldier called out "Stop!"

He walked over and pointed to Gittel and Lotte.

"Where did you get those dolls?" he asked Clara, trying to frighten her into saying something she shouldn't.

But Clara showed the same courage that her grandmother had when she'd made her own night crossing many years before.

"Oh, they're my *old* dolls, sir," she answered sweetly. "I've got much better ones at home, but Mama won't let me take them on trips because they could be ruined."

The soldier glanced at Mama, who wagged a finger at Clara and gave an

insincere smile. Then he stepped back, signaled the other guards to let them pass, and allowed the family to cross the border into free Switzerland.

Epilogue

By 1940, the war in Europe was raging, and the family had made still another long journey, from Switzerland to their new home, in England.

Clara's father quickly found work at a British war plant that made timers for bombs, where his business skills were valued highly. Mama worked too, helping the families of British soldiers who went to fight the Nazis. The family had survived not only the Nazis in Austria but also the strict rationing of food and the Blitz, when Nazi planes bombed English cities.

Eventually the war ended. Life became more like it had been before the Nazi terror began.

But the family never again heard from Clara's grandmother. She had stayed behind in Austria, along with aunts, uncles, and cousins who'd been taken away by the Nazis and had never come back. It seemed that almost every Jewish family had lost contact with relatives in Germany or Austria or Poland or France or Italy. The horrors of the Nazi concentration camps like

Auschwitz, Dachau, and Treblinka began to appear in the English newspapers every day, sometimes with pictures taken by news photographers from England, America, or even the Soviet Union.

Though their parents tried to shield them from the terrible stories, Clara and Marta began to understand what had truly happened to the people like Mr. Duessel, the kosher baker who'd disappeared. They knew that Papa had been right all along about the Nazis, and they admired his difficult decision to flee Innsbruck, but they still thought of their home now and then.

Marta went to high school in England, where her marks were the highest in her class. Clara went to school, too, and though she made many friends, she couldn't help but remember Hilde. Some of her new friends were Jewish and some were not, but Jews in England didn't wear yellow stars on their coats to show the difference.

Their new home was comfortable, and they slowly began to replace many of the things they had left behind in Austria.

Still, the two silver candlesticks that stood on the mantel in the parlor were their most treasured possession.

In the years to come, when the candlesticks were used for the Sabbath or on a holiday, Clara's mother always propped up the two dolls, Gittel and Lotte, on a small chair near the table.

"To freedom," Clara's father would toast, first holding his glass of sweet wine in the direction of the dolls and then to where his daughters sat, "and to the courage required to keep it."

KAREN ACKERMAN

is the author of *Song and Dance Man*, illustrated by Stephen Gammell, winner of the 1989 Caldecott Medal. Her many other children's books include *Just Like Max* and *When Mama Retires*, which *School Library Journal* called "warmly described . . . conveys the fears, the frustration, the happiness, and the values of [a] strong family." She is the author of two middle-grade novels, *The Leaves in October*, an ALA Notable Book, and *The Broken Boy*, which was named a New York Public Library Best Book for the Teen Age. A poet and a playwright, she makes her home in Cincinnati, Ohio.

ELIZABETH SAYLES

has illustrated a number of picture books for children, including Susan Tews's *Nettie's Gift* and *Albie the Lifeguard*, by Louise Borden, as well as the forthcoming *Mollie and the Prince*, by Mary Pope Osborne. She lives with her husband in Nyack, New York.

DATE DUE

JUL 1 4 '98			
GAYLORD			PRINTED IN U.S.A.